Gladys
goes to
War

Written by **Glyn Harper**

Illustrated by **Jenny Cooper**

PUFFIN BOOKS

Gladys was not musical like her sisters.

Music did not interest her at all. Nor did sewing, dresses or pretty things.

"Your needlework is a disgrace!" her mother said.

Gladys just smiled at her.

Whenever she could, Gladys helped her brothers and their friends work on car engines.

Her mother was worried. "Just look at your dirty hands!"

Gladys didn't care about her hands. She liked getting them dirty.

"No one will want to marry a mechanic," her mother told her.

But someone did.

Gladys met William Henning, a young man who loved cars as much as she did. William taught Gladys to drive. It took her less than an hour to learn.

William and Gladys married in 1912. They set up a business in Auckland selling cars.

But then came . . .

. . . WAR. William enlisted, and so did Gladys's two brothers.
That same day, Gladys wrote to the Government and offered
her services as a motor driver.

Back came the reply:

> *This will be a short war and women will*
> *not be needed. If you want to help the war effort, you*
> *should stay at home and knit socks and balaclavas.*

But Gladys didn't want to stay at home and knit.

She wanted to go to war . . .

. . . and so she did.

In 1916, Gladys sailed to Egypt with the New Zealand Volunteer Sisterhood. William was stationed there as a soldier, and was waiting for her as she stepped off the ship.

"Hello, my dearest," he beamed. "I knew they couldn't keep you in New Zealand."

Gladys became an ambulance driver. She took wounded soldiers to the big hospital at Giza. The roads were very bumpy, but Gladys was a careful driver.

A grateful British pilot took Gladys for a ride in his plane.

"One day I will learn to fly," Gladys told him.

The pilot laughed. "Very few women have done it," he said,
"but I think you just might."

When William's battalion moved to France to fight the German Army, Gladys went to England. At first she worked in a hospital as a cleaner, but she really wanted to drive again. The gruff Sergeant Major in charge of the drivers would not let her. "You're a cleaner," he said, "and anyway, men are much better drivers."

One day the hospital was short of drivers. Gladys volunteered.

"If you put one scratch on the vehicle," said the Sergeant Major, "it's back to scrubbing hallways!"

Gladys just smiled as he marched away.

From that day on, Gladys picked up wounded soldiers arriving from France and Belgium and raced them to the hospital.

Some nights, the Germans dropped bombs on London. While most people took shelter, Gladys sat ready in her ambulance.

One day, Gladys received a letter from her mother. *London is too dangerous for you*, she had written. *Please come home to New Zealand*.

Gladys wrote back straight away. She explained that her work was too important and William needed her close by. She promised she would be very careful.

But this was a difficult promise to keep.

One night, Gladys was taking four wounded soldiers to the hospital. All at once sirens blared and plane engines rumbled overhead — louder than Gladys had ever heard before.

Then bombs were falling all around them. Fires leapt up. Windows exploded and a building collapsed.

With every blast, the soldiers groaned. Gladys knew she must keep driving. "I'll get us to hospital in one piece," she vowed . . .

. . . and she did.

By this time, Gladys had been an ambulance driver for nearly two years. It was beginning to seem as if the war would never end . . .

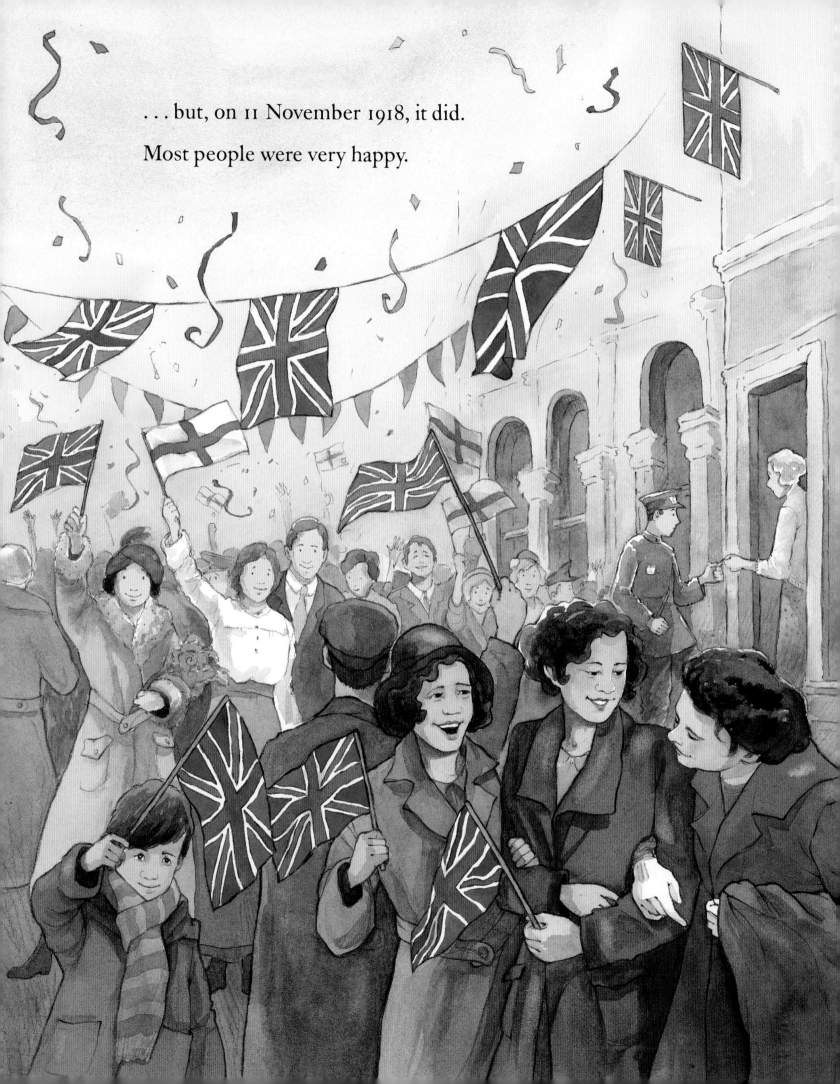

. . . but, on 11 November 1918, it did.

Most people were very happy.

It was not a good time for Gladys, though. First, she learned that both her brothers had been killed. Then she received a telegram. In wartime telegrams nearly always meant bad news.

This one was terrible. It said that William had been badly wounded and had died.

Worn out by the war and her sadness, Gladys became sick.

For weeks, she lay with a fever. She could barely breathe. Every bone in her body ached and her throat was so sore she couldn't eat.

She had influenza, a dangerous disease that had spread across the world and was killing millions of people. She got worse and worse. Finally the doctor said, "I don't think she'll live through the night."

But he didn't know Gladys.

In the morning she had improved. From that day on she slowly recovered from the 'flu.

For her war service, Gladys was given a medal called an M.B.E., an important honour granted by the King. The General in charge of all New Zealand soldiers in the United Kingdom wrote her a special letter of thanks for being such a skilled and capable driver.

When she was well again, Gladys was determined to do many things.

She wanted to go back to New Zealand and to travel across Australia.

She wanted to work with cars again.

She wanted to drive cars where no one else had ever driven them.

And she really wanted to learn to fly a plane . . .

The Amazing True Life of Gladys Sandford

Gladys was a real person and the events of this story really did happen. She achieved all this and a lot more in her lifetime. In a 1969 magazine interview she said:

> When I was young, women weren't supposed to do anything much, not even express themselves . . . For my own part, if I found a barrier, I just crashed through it.

Gladys Coates was born in Sydney, Australia, in 1891. When she was young her family moved to New Zealand, settling first in Auckland and then in Hawke's Bay.

In 1910, Gladys was working as a school teacher when she met William Henning. It was a real love match. William, a widower some years older than Gladys, admired her spirit and independence. They married, moved to Auckland and worked happily together in their car dealership.

Then came the Great War of 1914–18, and everything changed. Lieutenant William Henning, earlier awarded the Military Cross "for conspicuous gallantry and resource", died of wounds on 13 September 1918. Gladys's brothers did not survive the war either: Randolph died of wounds in Belgium in June 1917 and Eric died of pneumonia in Auckland in November 1918, just days before the war ended.

Devastated by her losses and exhausted from her war work, Gladys contracted the deadly influenza virus of 1918. While she did recover, the 'flu permanently damaged her lungs. Gladys would live with this for the rest of her life — another barrier to crash through.

Gladys remarried in 1920 to one of William's close friends, Squadron Leader Esk Sandford, an Australian serving with the Royal Air Force. The couple lived in England, India and Egypt. But the marriage did not work out and Gladys's lung condition worsened, so she returned to New Zealand alone in 1923. Spending almost a year in bed, Gladys was ordered to live a quiet life. But she was dreaming of cars and flying.

In 1924, Gladys became the first woman in New Zealand to work as a car sales representative. In 1925, after six and a half hours of instruction and two solo flights, she was the first woman in New Zealand to obtain a pilot's licence. Sadly, though, she never flew again after this, because flying was too expensive.

Gladys then embarked on another adventure, to drive across Australia east to west and north to south. On 4 March 1927, she set off with her friend Stella Christie, who could not drive, to attempt this feat. They encountered floods, impassable roads, crocodiles and snakes. The car repeatedly broke down, but Gladys made all the repairs. One time, in the middle of nowhere with a broken clutch, Gladys short-circuited the Transcontinental telegraph line. A repairman sent to locate the problem was very surprised to find the stranded women, but arranged for a new clutch to be sent. Gladys and Stella returned to Sydney on 25 July 1927, having driven a distance of 17,600 kilometres, and became the first women to make the crossings.

When the Second World War broke out, Gladys, now living in Sydney, played an active role. She was President of the National Emergency Service Drivers and also worked as a censor for the Army.

After the war, Gladys ran a poultry farm with a friend and worked for the Department of Repatriation. She retired in 1956 and moved into the War Veterans' Home at Narrabeen in Sydney, working tirelessly as an unpaid social worker for the New Zealand sub-branch of the Returned Services' League. She visited ex-New Zealand soldiers in hospital and assisted their families.

This remarkable woman died in 1971. There is no doubt that she lived a full, adventurous life and crashed through many barriers.